Nature's Circle

and Other Northwest Coast Children's Stories

Robert James Challenger

Copyright © 2004 Robert James Challenger
First Edition 2004

National Library of Canada Cataloguing in Publication

Challenger, Robert James, 1953-
        Nature's circle and other Northwest Coast children's
stories / Robert James Challenger. — 1st ed.

ISBN 1-894384-77-6

        1. Children's stories, Canadian (English) 2. Nature stories, Canadian (English) I. Title.

PS8555.H277N37 2004   jC813'.54   C2004-904718-3

Heritage House acknowledges the financial support for our publishing program from the Government of Canada through the Book Publishing Industry Development Program (BPIDP), Canada Council for the Arts, and the British Columbia Arts Council.

All illustrations: Robert James Challenger
Book design and layout: Darlene Nickull
Editor: Ursula Vaira

HERITAGE HOUSE PUBLISHING COMPANY LTD.
Unit #108 − 17665 66A Ave., Surrey, BC V3S 2A7

Printed in Canada

The Canada Council | Le Conseil des Arts
for the Arts | du Canada

BRITISH
COLUMBIA
ARTS COUNCIL
We acknowledge the support of the Province of British Columbia
through the British Columbia Arts Council

Dedication

This book is dedicated to Joannie Challenger, my companion for this journey around Nature's Circle.

Acknowledgements

The author acknowledges the following friends for their assistance and advice on the stories within this book.

Heather Owen, M.Ed.
District Counselling Psychologist
Sooke School District #62

Julie Wilmott, M.Ed.
Principal, Savory Elementary School
Langford, B.C.

Joannie Challenger, B.Ed.
Teacher, Hans Helgesen Elementary School
Metchosin, B.C.

Eagle's Reflection
and Other Northwest
Coast Stories
ISBN 1-895811-07-4

Orca's Family
and More Northwest
Coast Stories
ISBN 1-895811-39-2

Raven's Call
and More Northwest
Coast Stories
ISBN 1-895811-91-0

Salmon's Journey
and More Northwest
Coast Stories
ISBN 1-894384-34-2

All $9.95

Wonderful Northwest Coast stories for kids … Jim Challenger is a real artist as his book demonstrates.

—Shaw Cable's
"What's Happening?"

Modern day fables are the right length. … knows how to write for the oral storyteller; the written words slip easily off the tongue.

—Times Colonist

Clear images … brief, narrative style will appeal to young readers. Appropriate for read-aloud, … use the moral content to promote family values.

—Resource Links

Challenger's prose bears a deliberate resemblance to First Nation oral traditions: human and nature interact freely, and both are capable of folly, repentance, and wisdom. In his artwork, Challenger also embraces West Coast aboriginal culture by portraying his characters in exquisite Haida-style prints … returning to the stories is like returning to a favorite restaurant even after you have long ago memorized the menu. Highly recommended.

—Canadian Book Review Annual

Contents

The Circle Begins

Mother Eagle had been busy since the first spring weather arrived. She had worked on her nest by lining the inside with fresh moss and feathers. Shortly afterwards she laid two eggs and spent many days sitting on them to keep them warm. With her was Young Eagle, who had been born the previous spring. Now almost one year old, Young Eagle was starting to develop her white head feathers. Her wings were growing strong, and she had become a good hunter, catching most of her own fish from the nearby ocean.

As the sun rose on an early summer day, the eggs began to split open, and soon two new baby eagles were sharing the nest.

It was a very busy time for Mother Eagle. She now had to catch enough fish to feed her two growing babies. She no longer had time to go with Young Eagle to find food or to soar with her in the warm winds above their forest home.

Young Eagle was jealous of the two new eagles. They got all her mother's attention, and it made Young Eagle feel angry. One day, when she thought her mother wasn't watching, Young Eagle pecked at the young ones and stole their fish. The young ones cried out for their mother.

Mother Eagle screeched at Young Eagle, "Stop being mean to your brother and sister. Go off and practise your flying."

Young Eagle replied, "I don't want to practise flying all by myself. I want to go flying with you, but you never have time to go with me like you used to."

Mother Eagle said, "I think I know what's bothering you. You're angry because so much of my attention goes to the young ones that you think I have none left for you. I remember when your older brother felt the same way about you. But getting angry with your young brother and sister will not make things better. You could make things better by helping me take care of them. Then I'd have more time to spend with you."

Young Eagle asked, "What could I do to help you?"

Mother Eagle said, "Well, you are good at fishing, so what if you come with me and we'll both catch fish to feed all of us? That would save me a lot of time."

So off they went together, and in a short time they had caught enough fish to feed the four of them.

After they had all eaten, Mother Eagle said, "Thank you for your help, Young Eagle. Now I have some time before the sun sets to go flying with you."

Together they flew high up above their home, soaring in the warm evening breeze and watching the sun go down below the mountains off to the west.

Young Eagle said, "If I help you tomorrow can we do this again?"

Mother Eagle smiled at her and said, "Yes, we can. It's wonderful to have you as my helper."

Osprey's Fishing Game

The nest was high up near the top of an old spruce tree on the ridge overlooking the lake. In the nest were two young birds. They had been born early that spring and were now almost full grown. One bird had white tips on his wings, so Mother Osprey called him White Wings. The other bird was much darker, like his mother, so she called him Black Wings.

The two birds sat on the edge of their nest and watched fish rising in the calm waters of the lake below. Both of them loved to try to catch the biggest fish.

Black Wings took off from the nest and flew out over the lake. He called back to White Wings, "I bet I can catch a bigger fish than you can."

White Wings took off from the nest and said, "I bet you can't."

Black Wings spotted a trout feeding near the surface and dove straight down and splashed into the water above it. His sharp talons grasped the fish, and with a flap of his wings he took off, carrying his prize back to the nest.

White Wings saw him and was determined to catch a bigger fish. He saw a fish and dove down and picked it up. He flew back to the nest and compared his fish with Black Wings', but it was smaller.

Black Wings bragged, "I win. My fish is bigger than yours. I'm a better hunter than you are."

White Wings felt humiliated. He decided to go back out and catch a bigger fish. He flew over the water and soon spotted a huge fish. He dove down and grabbed it, but that's when things went wrong. White Wings thought he had caught the fish, but this fish was so big he couldn't lift it out of the water. The big fish started swimming toward the bottom and began to drag White Wings under the water.

Mother Osprey called out to him, "Let go, White Wings. Quickly!"

White Wings heard her and released his big fish. It swam away into the deep water. White Wings flew back to the nest and sat there, all dripping wet. He thought to himself, "Now Black Wings is really going to make fun of me. I'll never hear the end of it."

But instead Black Wings came over to him and said, "Are you all right? You could have been killed! And all over a stupid bet I made with you about who could catch the biggest fish. I'm sorry that I made fun of you."

White Wings felt better, and he said to his brother, "Thanks. I've learned that in any game, if you lose, you should not take it too seriously."

Black Wings nodded and said, "And I've learned that when you do win a game, you should be respectful to others and not brag about how good you are."

Old Kelp's Fronds

Mother said to Son, "Please take some of the berries we picked over to Grandmother and Grandfather's house."

Son replied, "I don't want to visit them. They're so old and they look creepy. Their skin is all brown and wrinkled and their hair is white as snow. Old Ones like them scare me."

Mother said, "Sit down and let me tell you a story about the Old Ones. Look out into the bay. See the big gardens of kelp fronds floating on the surface? Old Kelp has a long stem down to a strong anchor attached to a big rock.

"At the bottom of the ocean, Young Kelp is just beginning to grow. His anchor is not very strong yet, and he is not very tall. When there are big storms that send waves crashing into the bay, Young Kelp can't survive without Old Kelp's fronds to protect him and keep him safe.

"You see, Old Kelp learned from his parents how to keep the waves from tearing Young Kelp off the rocks. As the big waves come surging into the narrow bay, Old Kelp uses his strong anchor to hold on to the bottom as he catches the waves in his long fronds. Then he tosses each wave back out into the ocean, away from Young Kelp.

"Grandfather, Grandmother, and other Old Ones are just like Old Kelp. Don't be afraid of their wrinkled skin or white hair. They look like they do because they have lived for a long time, and that means they have lots of things that they can teach you."

Badger the Bully

Wolf and her cubs lived in a den that Wolf had dug out of a hillside the previous year. The cubs had been born there, and it was the only home they had ever known. The den was dry, even in the hardest spring rains, and the entrance was protected by a big stone that blocked the cold winds of winter.

One sparkling spring day, Wolf and her cubs went to explore along the river, looking for food and playing in the shallow pools. When they returned they were met at the entrance to their den by Badger.

Wolf said to Badger, "What are you doing here?"

Badger snarled back, "This is my den now. Go away and leave me alone."

Wolf said to Badger, "You are mistaken. This is the den that I dug last year, and this is where I raised my cubs. You can't just come in and take it."

Badger replied with a growl, "Yes I can, because if you try to take it back I'll bite you!" He crawled down inside the den.

Wolf didn't know what to do. She and the cubs needed a place to sleep, but she didn't want to get into a fight with Badger. If she got hurt, there would be nobody to protect the cubs. She decided to try another way.

Wolf called to Badger, "All right, you can have my den. But I hope you'll like having company for the winter."

Badger stuck his head out and said, "What company?"

Wolf smiled, "Black Bear doesn't have a den for this winter, so I told him that I would let him sleep in the back of my den. I'm sure you'll get to like him, even though he does snore a lot."

Badger said, "Oh. I don't want to share my den with Black Bear if he snores. Perhaps this isn't the best spot for me. But where can I find a new place?"

Wolf said, "Well, what if I helped you dig a new home over on the other side of the valley? Then you would have it all to yourself."

Badger looked down and said, "You'd do that for me, even though I tried to steal your den? Now I feel really bad. I'll try to be nicer to everyone from now on."

Turtle's Talents

I t was summer. The days were long and warm. The children were out of school, roaming around looking for something to do.

Raven watched some children standing near the pond. They were tapping something with a stick and shouting at it. Raven flew down to investigate and found the source of their amusement. It was Turtle.

Turtle was scared, so he had withdrawn into his shell to hide. The children were tapping on his shell with a stick to try and make him come out, but he wouldn't. They shouted at him, but that only made him more scared.

Raven asked the children, "Why are you being mean to Turtle?"

One of the older children replied, "We aren't being mean. We just want him to come out and play a game of tag with us."

Raven hopped onto Turtle's shell and peered inside. He said to Turtle, "Do you want to play with the children?"

Turtle responded, "I'd like to, but they run so fast, and I'm so slow that I can't keep up with them. I'm only quick when I'm swimming."

Raven looked up and asked the children, "How about if you try a swimming game with Turtle?"

The children cheered, and soon they were all swimming in the pond. Turtle might have been slow on land, but in the water he could swim very fast, so they all had a great game of water tag. When they finished playing they all sat on the rocks in the late-afternoon sunshine to warm up.

One of the children said to Turtle, "We are sorry that we were mean to you earlier. We didn't know we were scaring you. Will you play tag with us in the pond again tomorrow?"

Turtle smiled, "I would like that very much."

Raven smiled too and said to the children, "Turtle may not be able to do all the things that you can do, but if you are nice to him, you will discover he has talents that you don't even know about."

Arbutus Tree's Roots

It was a beautiful summer day with warm winds sailing white clouds across the blue sky. A young girl walked along the path above the beach. Waves crashed onto the rocks below, and their noise drowned out the sound of her sobbing. High above her, Eagle soared on the air currents. Eagle sensed the little girl's sadness and gracefully flew down and landed in Arbutus Tree just above where she stood.

The girl looked up at Eagle. She was beautiful, but her face was quite different from the other children who lived in the village. It was rounder and her skin was darker. She had deep brown eyes and her dark hair was full of long curls.

Eagle asked, "Why are you crying on such a beautiful day?"

The girl replied to Eagle, "I just moved here with my family from my home in the next valley. I had to leave all my old friends behind. When I went to school this morning, I had hoped to find some new friends, but instead they all just laughed at me and called me names. They wouldn't let me play their games."

Eagle asked, "Why do you think they did that?"

She answered, "They said that I look different from them. They all have lighter skin and no curls in their hair. I wish I was more like them."

Eagle said, "Why would you want to be like them? They should be wishing they could be more like you, because it's you that is the special one. Let me tell you a story to show you that being different also means that you are special.

"In the forest there is a tree called Cedar. She has many brothers and sisters and they all look the same. They all have light-brown bark, thin branches and shallow roots. Here, on the rocky shoreline you find Arbutus Tree living. Arbutus Tree has dark-brown bark, thick winding branches and deep roots.

"Long ago when Arbutus Tree tried to grow in the forest, cedar trees made fun of her dark bark and her curled branches. Cedar trees spread their branches out over the forest and wouldn't let Arbutus Tree have enough sunlight. Arbutus Tree asked me for help, so I picked her up and brought her to the shoreline, away from where cedar trees grow. Here she had lots of sunlight, but the soil was poor, so she had to push her roots deep down into the earth. The wind blew most of the time, so her big branches grew in strong, graceful curves.

"One winter a big storm came in from the ocean. Arbutus Tree had her deep roots and strong branches, so she survived. But the cedar trees had shallow roots and thin branches. Many of their branches broke off, and some trees almost fell over when their roots started to lift out of the ground.

"The cedar trees called out to Arbutus Tree, 'Help us. Our roots are coming out of the ground. When the next storm comes, some of us will blow down for sure.'

"Arbutus Tree replied, 'Why don't you hold each other up?'

"'We all grew the same shallow roots and weak branches, so we can't hold each other up,' replied a cedar tree. 'You are different because you have deep roots that the wind can't tear out of the ground and strong branches that won't break. We need help from someone special like you.'

"Arbutus Tree agreed to help the cedar trees. She spread her branches out, and in the next storm she caught the wind with them before it could blow into the forest. Her special roots, which only she had, held her upright in even the strongest gusts of wind. It was then that the cedar trees realized they couldn't survive without the unique ones among them."

Eagle looked at the little girl and said, "When you came from far away you brought games with you that the other children don't know about yet. When you go back to school tomorrow, you should teach them your games. Soon, they will see that you are special."

Little Orca

It was early in the morning when Grandfather and Grandson walked out of the house and down to the dock where Grandfather's boat was tied up. They loaded their fishing rods and lunch into the boat and set off toward the deep water off the point.

When they arrived Grandfather slowed the boat down and asked, "Do you want me to show you how to let out your line and how to reel in a fish when you get one?"

Grandson said, "No, I'm big now, so I know how to do it."

Grandfather smiled but didn't say anything.

Soon afterwards Grandson said, "I have a fish on my line!"

Grandfather stopped the boat and Grandson started to reel in his line. He kept getting the line tangled up on the reel, and by the time he got his hook to the boat, his fish had gotten away. Grandfather said to him, "Are you sure you don't want some lessons?"

Grandson said, "No, I'm too big to get lessons."

Grandfather started the motor again. A few minutes passed and Grandson said, "I have another fish!"

This time he pulled so hard that he broke the line, and his fish got away again.

Grandson said, "I don't understand why I can't catch a fish. I'm almost as big as you are, but my fish always get away."

Grandfather said, "Let me tell you the story about Little Orca. It will help you understand that being grown up has very little to do with how big you are.

"Little Orca was born one winter long ago. He and his mother swam with the other whales in Grandfather Orca's pod. One day the whales found a big school of salmon that were heading back to their river to spawn. Little Orca saw Grandfather Orca slowly swim into the school and quickly come out with a salmon in his teeth. Little Orca thought it looked easy to do, so he asked Grandfather Orca, 'I'm pretty big now, so can I try to catch a salmon?'

"Grandfather Orca said, 'Yes, you can, but first do you want me to teach you how it is done?'

"'No,' said Little Orca. 'I'm big, I can do it.' Off he went at full speed into the school of salmon. As soon as the salmon saw him coming, they started to race off in all directions. Little Orca chased them this way, then that way. Up and down and all around he went until he was too tired to swim anymore. Little Orca never even came close to catching a fish. All he did was scare them all away.

"Grandfather Orca said to him, 'Now you see that being grown up is more than just about how big you are. It is also about how much you have learned from others as you grew. Whenever you have the chance, let us show you how things are done. That's how you'll grow up some day.'

Grandfather said to Grandson, "Now, would you like some lessons on how to catch a fish?"

Grandson smiled at him and said, "Yes. If I'm ever going to grow up like Little Orca did, then I better get started now."

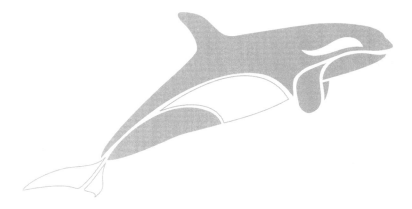

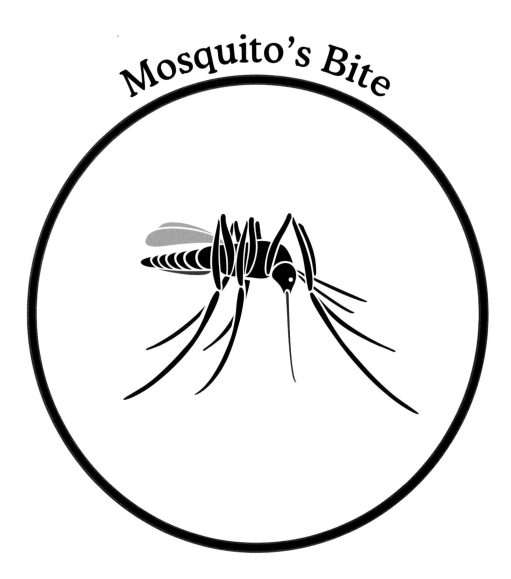

Mosquito's Bite

Granddaughter walked along the side of the road. She was crying, and her tears ran down her face and splashed onto the dry dust. She sat down on a stone beside the creek, closed her eyes, and let the sound of the water surround her, hoping it would wash away her sadness.

Mosquito, who lived in the wet grass alongside the creek, saw her and flew over to see if he could sneak up and get a meal from the unsuspecting girl. He landed on her arm and was about to have lunch when the girl's eyes opened, and she saw him about to bite her.

As she raised her hand to swat Mosquito, he called out, "Wait! I wasn't going to bite you. I just came over to see if I could help. Tell me why you are crying."

Granddaughter stopped. She wasn't sure if she could trust Mosquito, because in the past he had given her lots of itchy bites.

Granddaughter said, "I have a friend at school. I gave her a necklace made out of shells for her birthday. This morning she told me that she went swimming and lost the necklace. I am very angry with her, because she wasn't careful with the necklace. So if you want to help me, then go and bite her."

Mosquito jumped at the chance to avoid being swatted by Granddaughter and flew off to find the other girl.

Granddaughter laughed and said to herself, "She deserves every bite she gets."

The next day at school her friend showed up with a big bandage around her arm. Granddaughter had expected to see a bite mark or two from Mosquito, but this looked serious.

Granddaughter asked her friend, "What happened to your arm?"

Her friend replied, "I got a bite from Mosquito last night, and I scratched it. It got infected, and this morning it is all red and swollen. It really hurts."

Granddaughter felt bad. She had wanted to get revenge, but she hadn't wanted to hurt anyone. Instead of feeling better, now she felt even worse. She said to her friend, "It's my fault. I sent Mosquito to bite you, because I was angry at you for losing the necklace."

"I know you sent Mosquito to get me," said her friend. She peeled off the bandage. There wasn't a mark on her arm. It had been a trick!

"I caught Mosquito about to bite me, so he confessed about how you were looking for revenge. You should not have been so angry with me. I didn't mean to lose the necklace. It was an accident."

Granddaughter said, "I'm sorry that I tried to get revenge. My feelings were hurt, but thinking that I hurt you didn't make me feel any better. It made me feel even worse.

"After school, let's go down to the swimming pond, and this time instead of looking for revenge I'll help you look for your necklace."

Pheasant's Rings

Grandmother was doing the Christmas baking in the kitchen of the old house. Outside, the winter snows were blowing, and drifts almost covered the fence posts around the garden.

Grandson sat at the kitchen table, doing his homework. He had started learning how to read and was supposed to have his book read by the time school started again after the holiday. He was tired of reading, and he put down his book and said to Grandmother, "Is there something that I can help with?"

Grandmother smiled and said, "Well, how about if I make the dough and you cut out the cookies with the cookie cutters?"

Grandson pulled his chair over to the counter and began to help Grandmother cut out the cookies. When they finished, Grandmother put them into the oven to bake. Grandson then washed up the dishes they had used and put them away. He even swept up some flour that had dropped on the floor.

While the cookies were baking, he went back to the table and started reading again. One part of the story had a lot of big words that he didn't know. He asked Grandmother, "Would you help me with some of these words? I don't know what they mean."

Grandmother said to him, "Yes, I'd be happy to help you since you have so many rings on your tail."

Grandson looked puzzled and said, "What do you mean that I have rings on my tail? I don't have a tail."

Grandmother laughed and sat down beside him and said, "I was thinking about the story of how Pheasant got his rings. Every time Pheasant helps someone, he gets another ring for his tail. But every time he has to ask for help, he has to give back a ring from his tail. Pheasant hadn't helped any of his friends for a long time. His friends had asked for help, but Pheasant had always come up with an excuse, so he ran out of rings on his tail.

"Then it happened. Pheasant was out looking for food and got his foot tangled up in some blackberry vines. Pheasant called out for his friend's help.

"His friend came over and said, 'I don't know if I should help you. You don't have any rings to give me. Maybe I should leave you stuck here all night.'

"Pheasant realized that if he expected others to come to help him, then he'd better make sure that he always had lots of rings saved up.

"Pheasant said to his friend, 'I'm sorry. I will help you build a new nest tomorrow.'

"Pheasant's friend helped him get his foot free. The next day Pheasant helped him build his nest as he had promised. From that day on, whenever Pheasant had the opportunity he would help someone. Soon his tail was full of rings, and he never had to worry about asking for help when he needed it."

Grandmother smiled at Grandson and said, "Today you helped me make cookies and clean up the kitchen. You are always a good helper, so you have lots of rings to spare. That's why I am happy to help you with your reading."

Raven's Shadow

Two bear cubs tumbled and ran through the long summer grass, chasing the shadow of Raven, who was flying overhead. Raven would turn just before they caught his shadow, and the two cubs would have to run as fast as they could to catch up with it again.

Finally, Boy Bear Cub caught Raven's shadow and held one end of it down with his paws. Girl Bear Cub caught up and held the other end. With the two young bears standing on his shadow, Raven couldn't fly away.

Girl Bear Cub said to her brother, "Give me Raven's shadow. It should be mine."

Boy Bear Cub replied, "No. It's mine because I caught it first."

Raven said to both of them, "Pardon me, but my shadow belongs to me."

The cubs replied, "Not anymore. We have it now, so it is ours."

Raven frowned and said, "You may be holding on to it right now, but it is not yours."

They didn't listen. Girl Bear Cub tried to take the shadow away from her brother. She knocked him off the shadow, but when she did, she stepped off it too. Raven flew to a nearby tree, taking his shadow with him.

Raven said to the cubs, "Both of you need to learn that holding something doesn't mean it is yours. If you steal something, you may think it is yours to keep forever. But the thing you stole still knows who it really belongs to, and so do you.

"Remember that something isn't worth very much to you if you have to spend all your time fighting to try and keep it, like you did with my shadow. No matter how hard you try, eventually it will get away and find its way back to its owner, just like my shadow did."

Red Squirrel's Secret

Grandfather was out walking along the beach with Grandson. They were enjoying the cool mist coming in off the sea, because it had been very hot earlier in the day.

Grandson said, "Mother wants me to give some of my toys to the new boy who just moved in across the road. He doesn't have any, because his house burned down last month and all his toys were lost. I know he doesn't have any, but why should I have to give him mine?"

Grandfather said, "Let me tell you the story about Red Squirrel, and then you'll be able to decide if you want to give up some of your toys.

"Red Squirrel and Grey Squirrel lived in two trees next to each other. Each of them was very careful to collect seeds and store them in their trees, so they would have lots to eat during the cold winter months.

"One early winter day they were both out for a walk when a thunderstorm moved over the area. A bolt of lightning struck Grey Squirrel's tree and burned it to the ground. When Grey Squirrel came back and saw what had happened, he thought that he would surely die, because all his food was gone and it was too late to gather any more.

"Red Squirrel said to him, 'You can sleep in my nest tonight. Tomorrow we'll find you a new home.'

"That night, while Grey Squirrel was sleeping, Red Squirrel went to an old oak tree nearby and worked for many hours fixing up an old nest inside the trunk. Then he carried over half his seeds and put them into the new nest. He finished just as the sun started to rise.

"When Grey Squirrel woke up he was very sad. He said to Red Squirrel, 'Even if we find a place for me to stay, I won't have anything to eat this winter.'

"Red Squirrel replied, 'I don't know why you are so worried. Why don't you just stay in the other nest?'

"'What other nest?' asked Grey Squirrel.

"'That one, over there in the old oak tree. Remember we used to play there when we were young?'

"Grey Squirrel ran over to the old oak tree and up into the nest. In a few seconds he stuck his head out and said with a big smile, 'It's perfect! It's like someone was just living here yesterday. There's even enough seeds for me to make it through the winter!'

"Red Squirrel smiled to himself and went back to his own nest."

Grandson asked, "Grey Squirrel never knew that it was Red Squirrel who had helped him?"

Grandfather replied, "That's why it felt so good for Red Squirrel. He knew that he had done a good deed, and it wasn't important that his friend knew who did it. It was only important that his friend was happy again."

Grandson thought about the story for a while, then said to Grandfather, "Tonight will you help me take some of my toys to my friend across the street? We can hide them in the tree fort in his yard."

Grandfather said, "But then he won't know that you gave him some of your toys."

Grandson smiled at him and said, "I know he won't. But I will."

Swallow Joins the Team

Eagle sat high up in his favourite tree, watching the world below him. It was springtime and lots of birds were busy building nests for their babies.

Hummingbird was building her nest in the branches of the old cedar tree. She was bringing moss from the edge of the pond, mixing it with dandelion seeds and spider's silk. Wolf was helping her by rubbing off his winter coat, so she could use the fine fur to line her cozy nest.

Crow was building her nest in a fir tree. She was weaving sticks together to form a basket, and she would soon start lining it with soft moss. Beaver helped her by felling small trees and nipping the branches into short lengths. Everyone was working together as a team.

Swallow hadn't started building her nest. She was just flying around and watching the others work. She had never built a nest before. She was afraid that the others might laugh if her nest fell apart or looked funny.

Eagle called out to her, "Aren't you going to start building your nest soon? If you don't, you won't have a place to lay your eggs."

Swallow answered, "I'm not sure how to get started. I've never built a nest before."

Eagle replied, "Well, the best way to learn is to help someone else build theirs."

Eagle called down to Hummingbird and Crow, "Hey! Swallow wants to help you build your nests. What can she do for you?"

Hummingbird said, "I could use some help bringing Wolf's fur to my nest. She could do that."

Crow said, "And when she's finished that, she could help bring moss to line my nest."

So Swallow joined the team, helping the others build their nests. Before they knew it, both Crow and Hummingbird's nests were done.

Crow said to Swallow, "Now let's get started on your nest. You said that you have never built one, so the first thing is to pick a place. It has to be safe and dry, like the inside of the old oak tree over there."

Hummingbird said, "Then you need to bring in twigs and grass to line it with, and fine fur to help keep your chicks warm when they hatch. I'll show you where there are lots of twigs over by the pond where Beaver trimmed the sticks for Crow's nest."

So off the three of them went, working together. Crow and Hummingbird taught Swallow how to build her nest and the three of them promised that next year they'd all help each other again.

Swallow was happy because she was now part of the team.

Wolverine's Rule

One warm summer day, Raven took a group of young animals on a walk through the forest to teach them the names of all the different plants that grew there. When they arrived at a small clearing, Raven told them to split up and try to collect as many different types of plants as they could.

Raven stayed with the younger animals so they wouldn't get lost, but the older animals went off on their own. All of a sudden there was a great commotion off in the woods. Raven and the young ones went to investigate.

When Raven arrived he found Wolverine and Wolf fighting. Wolf was biting Wolverine, and Wolverine was scratching Wolf. Both were snarling at each other and scaring all the others.

Raven calmly said, "Stop fighting and tell me what this is all about."

They stopped, and Wolf said, "Wolverine's cheating. When I told him that he wasn't following the rules, he bit me."

Raven asked, "What rules did he break?"

Wolf replied, "He was collecting plants that I'd already found."

Wolverine snapped, "That's what we are supposed to be doing."

Wolf snarled back, "No. The rule is that when one animal has found a plant, then nobody else can collect it. Isn't that the rule, Raven?"

Raven sighed to himself and said, "I don't recall making any rules at all. All I asked you each to do was collect as many different plants as you could."

Wolf said, "But what's the point of both of us bringing back the same plant?"

Raven replied, "You are right. We really only need one example of each type. Does anyone have an idea of how we should do that?"

Wolverine said, "How about if we all go out and collect them together? That way if one of us finds a certain plant, then we'll all know not to bring back another one."

Raven said, "So, let's make a rule that once one of you finds a certain plant, then nobody else should bring it in. Is that all right with everyone?"

All of them agreed to the new rule.

Raven said, "Good. You see, it's much better to settle things without fighting. Fighting only makes things worse. Next time, we all need to make sure everyone understands and agrees to the rules before we start, so there won't be any more fights."

Ladybug's Little Spots

Granddaughter sat on the porch of the house. The warm days of summer had finally arrived, and the garden was in full bloom. Flowers were stretching their arms out to catch the sunlight that flowed down from the sky.

Granddaughter seemed to be by herself most of the time. She would often sit on her porch and watch the other children play games. She wanted to play too, but because she was so small she was scared to join in.

Granddaughter saw a little red insect crawling across a leaf in the garden below her. She hopped down off the porch to see what it was. It was very small and shiny, with little black spots that looked like eyes.

Granddaughter asked, "What is your name?"

The insect replied, "My name is Ladybug."

Granddaughter asked, "How come I've never seen you in the garden before?"

"Oh, I've been here all along, but I'm small and I usually stay under the leaves, out of sight," said Ladybug.

Granddaughter said, "You're kind of like me. I've always been the smallest of all the children around here, so I like to hide too."

Grandmother had come out of the house, and she walked over to where the two were talking. She said to Granddaughter, "Ladybug has lived in my garden for a long time. She is usually off by herself, but she doesn't need to hide. She is small, but has the courage of a giant.

"For example, one day Bird came and began to eat all the ripe vegetables in my garden. He pecked holes in the tomatoes and gobbled down my gooseberries. I tried to shoo him away, but he just kept coming back. Ladybug was worried. If Bird ate up all the garden, then she wouldn't have a place to live. And I was worried that if Bird ate everything, then I wouldn't have any vegetables to eat.

"Ladybug came to the rescue. She climbed out from under the leaves and onto a tomato, right in front of Bird. She raised her spotted wing covers, and to Bird it looked like the tomato had suddenly grown eyes. Bird was a bit scared, because he'd never seen a tomato with eyes. Then the tomato started to talk, which really frightened him!

"Ladybug said, 'How would you like it if I came to your house and ate all your food?' That was enough for Bird. He knew he was wrong and apologized for eating the food that was not his. He promised never to do it again and flew off to find his own food.

"I said to Ladybug, 'Thanks for helping to save my garden. You were very brave.'"

Grandmother said to Granddaughter, "Don't let your size keep you from playing with your friends. They will soon see that it is the little ones, like you, who often show the most courage when it is needed."

Snow Goose Finds a Friend

Snow Goose had been out looking for a home when she was caught in an early fall snowstorm. She bravely flew on, fighting the wind and cold. But as the night came it got colder, and the snow built up on her wings until the weight was finally too much and she had to land. She felt that she would never find a home now. As the snow continued to fall, she was soon covered up.

The next morning a little girl came out of her house and looked across the fresh snow. She decided to try and find a friend to play with. As she walked down the path, she was puzzled by a lump of snow out in the field. She didn't recall it being there yesterday, so she went to investigate. She carefully dug down and discovered the frozen bird. She was sure Snow Goose was dead. Tears came rolling down her face onto the frozen feathers.

Raven heard the little girl crying and flew over to her. He looked at Snow Goose and knew that she needed the warmth of a friend. From the little girl's tears, he also knew that she had a gift of caring and that she needed a friend too.

Raven said to the little girl, "Look, your warm tears are bringing Snow Goose back to life."

Sure enough, where her tears had landed on the frozen white feathers, they had melted away the ice. Snow Goose stirred and opened her eyes and smiled at the little girl.

The little girl said, "Don't worry, you have a home now. I'll take care of you." She carried Snow Goose back to the house and showed her to Grandmother.

"Look, I found Snow Goose out in the field," she said to Grandmother.

Grandmother looked at the beautiful white bird that her granddaughter had saved and said, "Looks like you've found a friend. Or perhaps it was Snow Goose who found a friend, just when she needed you most."

The Circle Begins Again

Wolf stood alone on the ridge top as the moon rose from behind the mountain range. He let out a long sad howl that echoed down to the valley below.

Eagle heard it and flew up to where Wolf sat. Eagle landed beside him and said, "I heard that your grandfather recently died. He was a good friend to me for many years. It is natural for us to feel sad."

Wolf said, "I miss him. I'm afraid of being alone without him to help me and tell me what to do."

Eagle said, "I think he will still be there to guide you when you really need him."

Wolf gave Eagle a puzzled look and asked, "How can he still be here? He's dead."

Eagle replied, "When someone dies, they are still here, but in a different way. Remember when Grandfather used to tell you stories when he came to visit? After he left and went back home, didn't you still have those stories in your head?"

"Yes," said Wolf. "I remember all the stories he told me."

"Well," said Eagle, "do you remember the one he told you about the time he tried to cross the river on a rotten log, but it sank?"

Wolf laughed out loud. "Yes, I do. Grandfather had to swim back to shore, and when he got home he had to explain to Grandmother why he was all wet. It was very funny."

Eagle looked at Wolf. "See, that story still makes you laugh. It shows that he's still in your memory. When you feel sad and miss him, think about all the other stories he told you and about the things he taught you to do. That will remind you that even though someone dies, they live on in the memories they leave behind."

About the Author

Born in Vancouver, British Columbia, in 1953, Robert James (Jim) Challenger now lives in Victoria, British Columbia, on the southern end of Vancouver Island.

Jim has spent his life absorbing all the stories that the Northwest Coast has to offer. A keen observer of the natural behaviour of wildlife, he has developed his own style of artwork that captures the essence of the animals, birds, and fish that live around him.

Jim is an accomplished artist and stone carver. He has sold his beach-stone carvings to collectors around the world. His form-line designs are highly sought because of the way they capture the shape and movement of his subjects while maintaining the simplicity of flowing lines and shapes.

Jim bases his writing style on the oral storytelling traditions of past generations. His original works weave uplifting messages into entertaining interactions between his characters. His four previous books are already used extensively by both parents and teachers to stimulate young children to talk about their experiences.